Night *of the* Five Aunties

Mesa Somer

Illustrations by Kate Salley Palmer

Albert Whitman & Company • Morton Grove, Illinois

Dedicated with love to my husband, Stuart, for his inexhaustible love, patience, and support. M.S.

For my mother and all her beautiful sisters. K.S.P.

The text is set in Sabon.
The illustrations are colored pencil and watercolor.
The design is by Karen A. Yops.

Text © copyright 1996 by Mesa Somer.
Illustrations © copyright 1996 by Kate Salley Palmer.
Published in 1996 by Albert Whitman & Company,
6340 Oakton Street, Morton Grove, Illinois 60053.
Published simultaneously in Canada by
General Publishing, Limited, Toronto.

Printed in the U.S.A.
10 9 8 7 6 5 4 3 2 1

Library of Congress Cataloging-in-Publication Data

Somer, Mesa.
Night of the five aunties / written by Mesa Somer;
illustrated by Kate Salley Palmer.
p. cm.
Summary: For the first time ever, all five aunts are
coming for a visit at the same time, and one of them
has something very important to announce.
ISBN 0-8075-5631-9
[1. Aunts—Fiction. 2. Family life—Fiction.] I. Palmer, Kate Salley, ill.
II. Title.
PZ7.S69623Ni 1996
[E]—dc20
95-32021
CIP
AC

Me and my brother, Alfie, have five aunties, all of them beautiful. Aunt Clarabelle, Aunt Annabelle, Aunt Flora Mae, Aunt Dora Mae, and Aunt Ruby Dee all have beautiful dark wavy hair that swooshes around their faces, and they wear beautiful dresses with big pink flowers and stockings that say "skish skish skish" when they walk, and they have beautiful sparkling rings and long dangling earrings. And each with a different smell, so when two or three aunties get together, it's like a Christmas of smells.

Two or three aunties were the most we ever had visit, until one day, all five aunties came. We'll never forget it. It started when Mom got a phone call.

"Ruby Dee is *what*?" We heard Mom yell, so me and Alfie crawled under the table, where we could listen in. "When is she going to tell him? What do you mean, she's not going to tell him? She has to tell him!"

Me and Alfie looked at each other. Aunt Ruby Dee was our favorite aunt, and the most beautiful. What was she supposed to tell? And to whom? It was a mystery.

Before we could hear anymore, Mom saw us under the table and made us leave. Five minutes later she danced into the room, grabbed Alfie, and whirled him around in the air.

"Annie! Alfie! Guess what?!" she shouted. "The aunties are coming! The aunties are coming!"

"Hooray!" we yelled. "Hooray!"

"*Which* aunties?" Dad asked. "*When*?"

"*All* the aunties!" Mom put Alfie down and grabbed my hands. "All five aunties are coming on Friday!"

Then, while Dad just shook his head and smiled, me and Mom and Alfie did a Conga Dance around the living room, chanting, "All five aunties are com-ING! All five aunties are com-ING! All five aunties are com-ING!"

We cleaned the house until there was nothing left but furniture. Outside, me and Alfie had to rake the leaves, and we made a man-high mountain of them in the backyard. It looked good.

On Friday we put on our best clothes and Mom put a roast in the oven. Dad even made a fire in the study fireplace for the first time ever, and just as he lit the match, the aunties arrived.

Aunt Clarabelle came first in a bright red car without any roof and a purple scarf tied around her hair. Alfie calls her our Smoosh Auntie because when she hugs him there is so much of her and so little of Alfie you can hardly see anything left of him while the hug is going on. She came with Uncle Walter, who gave us two big presents wrapped with red ribbons. We got an electronic bullhorn that changes your voice and clown face paint with twenty-five colors. Dad took them away and said we could play with them tomorrow.

Aunt Flora Mae and Aunt Dora Mae came next. Mom says they are the wild ones, which means they live together in the city and have lots of boyfriends. We call them our Chocolate Aunties because they always give Alfie and me big fancy chocolate bars in shiny wrappers.

"Yoo hoo," they sang, tumbling out of their minibus. "Yoo hoo! Annie! Alfie! Look what we brought for our favorite niece and nephew!" Aunt Dora Mae waved a chocolate bar. It was bigger than any chocolate bar I'd ever seen.

We went in the house, and the aunties were kissing everyone and each other about ten times each. Dad took away our chocolate bar (for *after* supper, he said) but Aunt Flora Mae winked and gave us a handful of chocolate kisses. We stood at the window to eat them so Dad wouldn't notice, and that's when we saw Aunt Annabelle and Uncle Leo and Aunt Ruby Dee and

Uncle Cooper drive up in Aunt Annabelle's big pink Cadillac. It rolled to the curb, and Aunt Ruby Dee popped out and ran up the lawn. Uncle Cooper got out and called to her, and Aunt Ruby Dee turned around, took off her shoe, and threw it right at him. Then she ran to our house, opened the door, and clomp, thub, clomp, thub, clomp, ran upstairs—crying!

In one minute all the aunties, and Mom, too, went clomp, clomp, clomp, clomp up the stairs after Aunt Ruby Dee. Uncle Cooper and Uncle Leo came in, and all the uncles and Dad shook hands and then just stood around with their hands in their pockets. Me and Alfie crept up the stairs to listen in on the aunties.

"OOooooooooo," Aunt Ruby Dee was crying in the hallway. The aunties were around her cooing and chirping like a flock of birds.

"There now."

"It's all right."

"Hush now."

Then one said, "You know, you have to tell him."

What did Aunt Ruby Dee have to tell? Me and Alfie crept a little closer.

"I *tried* to tell him. I *did*. I said some things might change in our life, and he said he *never* wants us to change and our lives are just *perfect,* and then I just *couldn't* tell him. Oooooooo."

Me and Alfie looked at each other. Why was Aunt Ruby Dee going to change?

"I tried to tell him in the car, and he turned on the *ball game*! And when I say we should talk, he says *later*!"

Aunt Annabelle spoke: "You know why, don't you? He's nervous because of all of us, that's why. Whenever we all get together, Leo says he feels like he's in a room with six firecrackers about to go off."

"Walter says he feels like he's in a jar with six wasps— and then someone shakes the jar," Aunt Clarabelle added.

Aunt Ruby Dee chuckled, and then all the aunties started laughing, and then they held onto each other, laughing "whoop whoop whoop!" and wiping their eyes. Me and Alfie looked at each other and shrugged. Sometimes we just don't understand the aunties. Then they stopped, and the purses and the tissues and the lipsticks came out, and they were all busy with little mirrors and powder and stuff.

"There now, how do I look?" Aunt Ruby Dee looked around and saw me and Alfie. "Am I a fright?" she asked us.

Alfie shook his head. "You're better than the Fourth of July," he said.

The aunties' faces kind of crumpled and they all moaned "*Awwww.*" Then they were on Alfie in a flash, kissing him and hugging him, and then me, too, and I think we got about ten years of huggings and kissings in just that minute.

Uncle Cooper was standing at the bottom of the stairs when we tromped down again. "You all look like the Miss America pageant," he said, looking at Aunt Ruby Dee like she was the only one in the room. The way she smiled back at him you knew she wasn't mad anymore.

Then the smoke alarm went off and everyone saw the smoke pouring out of the kitchen.

"The roast!" Mom yelled.

The uncles and Dad rushed into the kitchen. The aunties rushed in after. We couldn't see anything because of the smoke.

Everyone was yelling. Dad pushed by us with the fire extinguisher, and we heard a big hiss. When the smoke cleared Aunt Clarabelle held up the black, burned roast so we could all see.

"Anyone for pizza?" Dad asked.

Before anyone could answer, the room suddenly filled up with firefighters.

Four firefighters pushed into the kitchen, a ladder clattered against a window, and we heard clomp, clomp, clomp up the stairs. More firefighters ran by us down the hall, toward the study. Aunties were shouting at the firefighters and the firefighters were yelling at us. Aunt Clarabelle waved the roast in the air. Then we saw a firefighter open the door to the study, and big clouds of white smoke came pouring out!

Dad grabbed me and Alfie and ran outside with us. The aunties and everyone ran right behind, and we all stood on the sidewalk, waiting for the house to burn up. Then a fireman came out and walked up to Dad.

"Sir, next time you use your fireplace, try to remember to open the flue." That meant the house wasn't going to burn up. There wasn't any real fire at all. Me and Alfie were a little disappointed at first, but the firefighters let us put on their hats and sit in their truck and make the lights go around. Two of the firefighters stayed for a long time, talking and laughing with Aunt Flora Mae and Aunt Dora Mae. When they finally left they gave me and Alfie firefighter badges. Aunt Flora Mae and Aunt Dora Mae got firefighter badges, too.

After the firefighters left, the pizza girl came, and we ate. Then Dad and the uncles went to watch the game, while the aunties "got comfortable" in the dining room. That meant they took off their shoes and talked about everything in the world, while me and Alfie listened in under the table. We were waiting for them to talk about the mystery. It was dark under the table, but all around us were beautiful auntie toes, a rainbow of toes, red and orange and pink and purple.

"I've been thinking, Ruby Dee, and I know just how you should tell Cooper," Aunt Clarabelle said.

Me and Alfie listened hard.

"What you should say is—"

"Oh, look!" Mom said suddenly. "It's snowing out! The first snow of the season!"

Everyone looked, and that's why we all saw Uncle Cooper drop out of the sky.

"Cooper?" Aunt Ruby Dee said. Then she screamed, "COOOPER!"

Aunties went running out the front door. The uncles and Dad came yelling out the side door. Everyone ran around the house and found a policeman standing over Uncle Cooper, who was lying on top of me and Alfie's leaf mountain. Aunt Ruby Dee rushed to his side. The policeman was talking into his walkie-talkie.

"Suspect down. Will need an ambulance, over?"

"Suspect?!!" Aunt Ruby Dee yelled.

"That's right, ma'am. A neighbor reported a suspicious man climbing up the back of your house."

"That's no suspect, that's my husband!"

Dad explained to the policeman that Uncle Cooper was just trying to change the antenna so they could get better reception on the game. Then the ambulance came, and the ambulance woman stared into Uncle Cooper's eyes with a little flashlight and asked him a lot of questions, and then he was standing up, saying, "I'm all right, I'm fine, I'm fine."

"Sir, you're real lucky. From that height, you could've broken your neck," the ambulance woman said. "You ought to thank whoever put that leaf pile right there."

"That was Annie and Alfie," Dad said.

Uncle Walter came up and put a hand on my shoulder. "Well, Annie, you and your brother may have saved your uncle's life."

And in a flash, the aunties were around us again, calling us heroes, and we got *another* ten years of huggings and kissings, and when they were done Alfie looked like a leopard with red and pink lipstick spots all over, and I guess I did, too, because everyone looked at us and started to laugh.

It was dark by that time, and the snow was coming down in big white flakes. We all stood on the back porch, watching the snow. Aunt Ruby Dee took Uncle Cooper inside to put a Band-Aid on a scrape. From the back porch you can see right into the kitchen window, so we could see Aunt Ruby Dee kissing Uncle Cooper's finger. Then they were just talking back and forth, and suddenly Uncle Cooper picked up Aunt Ruby Dee in his arms and whirled her around and around. He put her down and kissed her just like in the movies, and then he opened the window and yelled:

"We're going to have a baby!"

When Aunt Ruby Dee and Uncle Cooper came out to the porch again, Aunt Clarabelle shouted, "Conga Dance!"

"Conga Dance!" all the other aunties shouted. We made a long line, the aunties and the uncles and Dad and Mom and us, and we danced and kicked, the aunties still in their bare feet, back and forth across the backyard, chanting, "A brand

new baby is com-ING, A brand new baby is com-ING!
A brand new baby is com-ING!" A newspaper reporter
showed up, saying he wanted a story about the house where
the firefighters, the police, and the ambulance had all been
called in one day, and he took a picture of us dancing in the
snow in the moonlight. It was on the front page of the
newspaper the next day.

Cousin Maybelline was born the next summer. Mom gave her my old baby clothes, and Aunt Ruby Dee lets me and Alfie hold her if we sit very still on the couch. Since Aunt Annabelle moved to California, and Aunt Dora Mae got married to the firefighter, we hardly see more than one auntie, sometimes two, at a time. But when cousin Maybelline gets old enough, I'm going to tell her all about the Night of the Five Aunties.